TO The Hinton Family
Katu Crawford Allen
2021

WHAT THE MAP LEFT OUT

WRITTEN AND ILLUSTRATED BY
KATIE CRAWFORD ALLEN

ISBN: 978-1-954614-30-7 (hard cover)
ISBN: 978-1-954614-31-4 (soft cover)

Editing: Amy Ashby

Published by Warren Publishing
Charlotte, NC
www.warrenpublishing.net
Printed in the United States

*To everyone who has believed in me
(especially my husband). This is for y'all!*

We have felt a growing call
from the map upon our wall.
We stuck a pin just to show
exactly where we want to go.

With a string stretched extra tight
for the fastest route in sight,
we hurry quickly to the door
to see precisely what's in store.

But if a wrong turn in the dark
makes us miss our mark,
we don't need to change pace.
It's not meant to be a race.

When the path can't be found,
we'll take a pause and look around.
Someone's there to lend a hand
and get us back to where we planned.

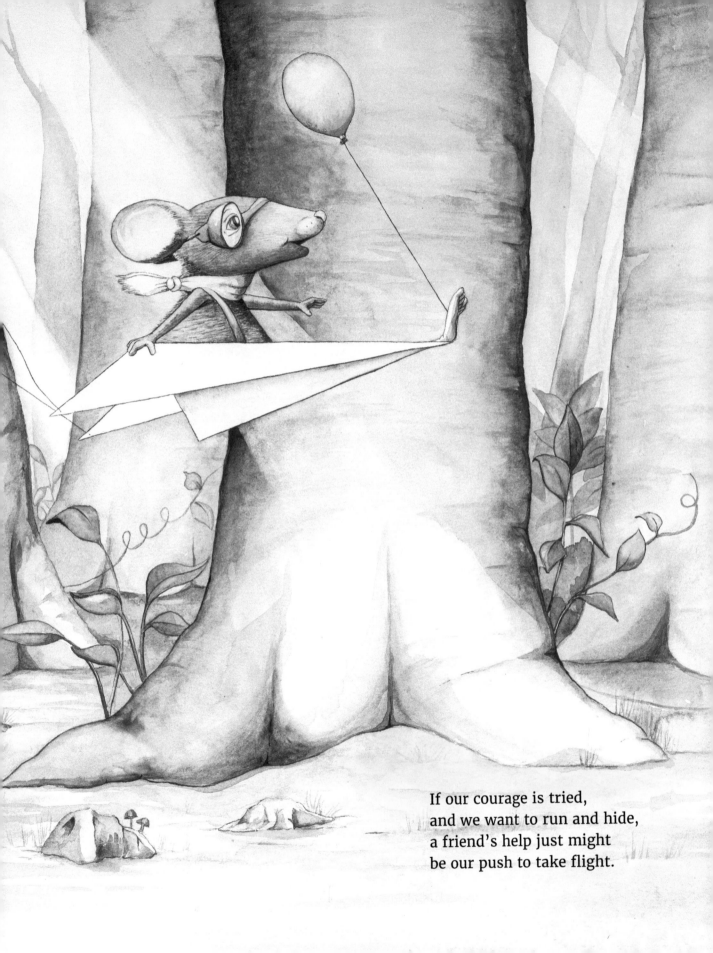

If our courage is tried,
and we want to run and hide,
a friend's help just might
be our push to take flight.

But sometimes unseen forces
can affect the bravest courses.
So if we still land in a maze,
it might be time to try new ways.

And when those ways prove clear,
let that steady friend steer.
It doesn't need to be our boat
if it's keeping us afloat.

Enjoy the smooth sailing,
but take time to help those ailing,
(even when the current's fast
and it's easier to float on past).

In that pause to be kind,
it's possible to grow our minds.
It's hard for us to smell a rose
if our pace never slows.

So when toes are toasting
and marshmallows roasting,
enjoy the rest.
We need it to be our best.

Once refreshed from the break,
make sure everyone's awake.
Take a stretch, greet the day,
check the map, and plan a way!

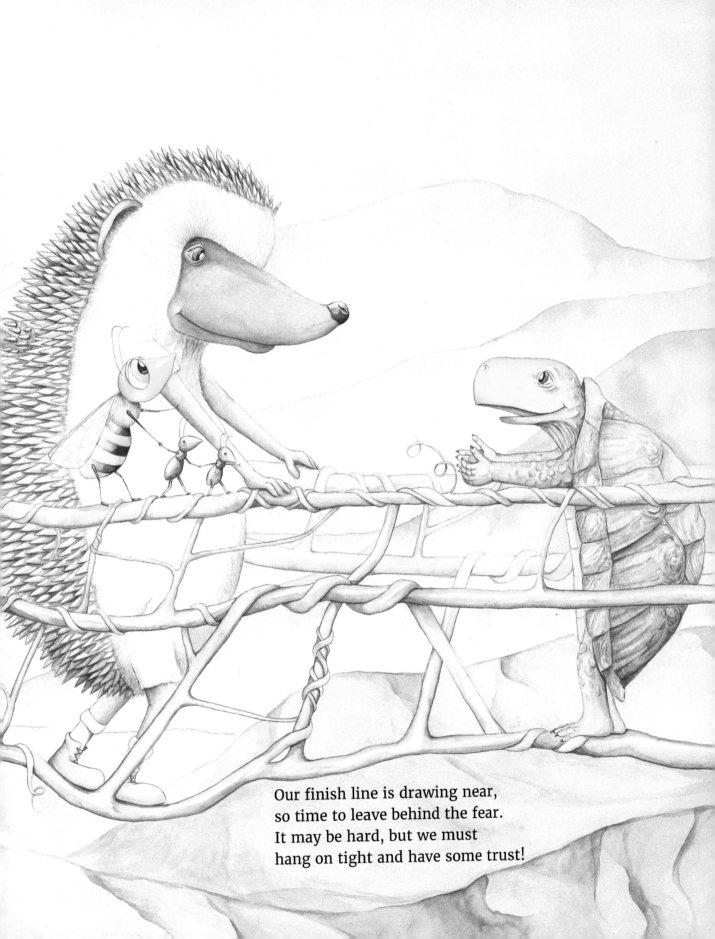

Our finish line is drawing near,
so time to leave behind the fear.
It may be hard, but we must
hang on tight and have some trust!

We've held our course to the end,
found exactly where we pinned.
But this place that we sought
Isn't quite what we thought.

How could we know at the start
our map was missing the best part?
The greatest win was who we met,
not the destination set!

So when we look around and see
friends dancing with us gleefully,
let's put down the map, our journey's done.
We have made it! We have won!

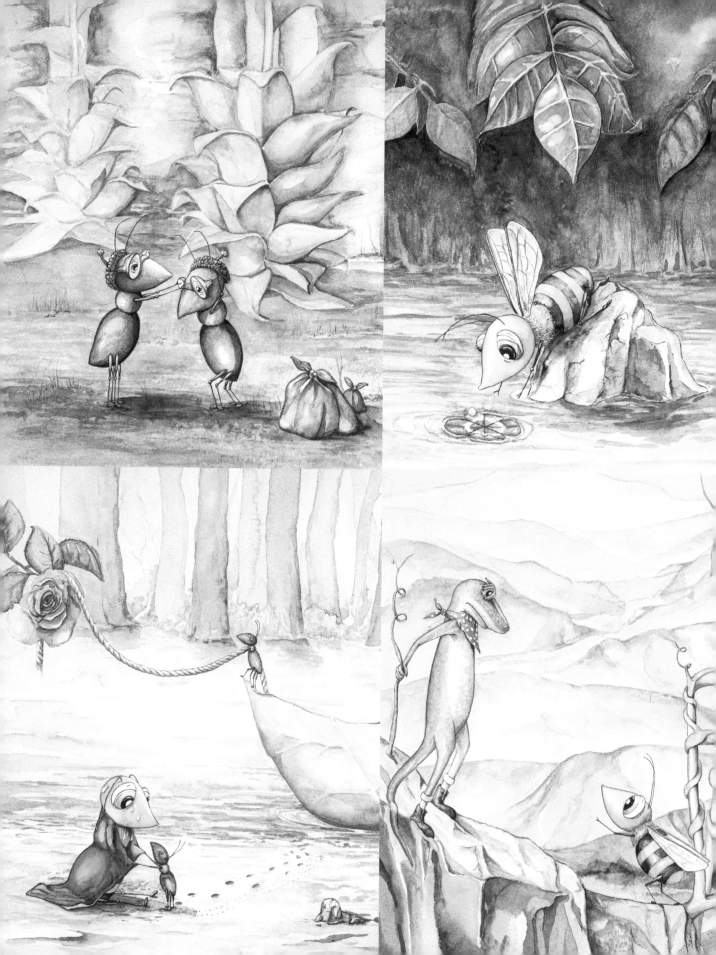

CPSIA information can be obtained
at www.ICGtesting.com
Printed in the USA
LVHW071023070821
694747LV00002B/4

9 781954 614307